PARALYZED

WHEN YOU GET AND WHEN YOU LOSE

SHRYESTHA PUTATUNDA

To myself,

"I am proud of you for surpassing your own expectations."

Lorose

Keep it up.

Contents

Preface *vii*

Acknowledgements *ix*

Prologue *xi*

1. Daiki Nakamura 1
2. Ashahi Minamoto 5
3. The Smile Unknown 10
4. To Be Needed 13
5. Lies 17
6. Silhouette That Stays 22
7. To Be Free 27
8. The First Photo 31
9. Paralyzed 36

Preface

None of the incidents that has taken place in this book is real. It is completely my imagination.

To be honest, I don't know what made me want to write a book like this. The year 2020 was a blast of emotions for me. I was too overwhelmed. That was when I had the sudden urge to write this story. I always like my stories to be impactful. Hopefully this story will leave an impact on all who reads it.

Even now when I am writing this preface, my mother is cooking just behind me. Smells so delicious!

Preface

None of the [illegible] that has taken place in this book is [illegible] real. It is completely my imagination.

To be honest, I don't know what [illegible] want to [illegible] write a book like [illegible]. The year 2020 [illegible] of [illegible] emotions [illegible] were being [illegible] had [illegible] write this [illegible] story [illegible] the [illegible] fully [illegible]

[illegible]

[illegible]

Acknowledgements

I would like to thank myself who never gave up on her dreams and continued to write what her heart desired. It's not easy to not give up. So I am proud of myself who never gave up no matter how hard things became.

Prologue

As I am looking up at the sky, I can see no stars.

Not that I care.

For me it has always been like that. I have already accepted that and care no more. As long as I can continue to hold this darkness within me, I will be alive. The moment I let it go, I will be dead for darkness is all that I have left within me.

People say that a lie when told continuosly can become the truth. I wonder if that really is the case...

CHAPTER ONE

Daiki Nakamura

I hate everything.

I hate my parents. I hate my brother. I hate my relatives. I hate this world.

But what I hate the most is myself... I hate myself for being who I am... for wanting something I can never achieve...

Daiki Nakamura. My name Daiki refers to a child who shines brightly. What an absolute lie-

Not a single part of me is worth shining.

As I am sitting in the last bench of my class while staring out of the window and waiting for the class to end, I feel nothing. Today is supposed to be the last day of our school. Soon everyone reading in this class will enter college. As i look around in the class, I see everyone giving their final farewells to each other. Some of them are even tearing up.

What nonsense-

Nothing will change even in the college. Everyone will eventually forget everything. I don't see any reason to tear up.

As I got up and left the class a boy kept on following me until I turned around and asked him what he needed from me. He seemed to be a little nervous at first. After a few seconds of silence he said, "Today is the last day... We were thinking of holding a farewell party for ourselves... Since you are a part of our class... will you join us?"

His words annoyed me. A party for what? Since they will be graduating? Do they really don't understand that their lives are going to become harder from here on out?

"I have no reason to attend such a party. And I would suggest you-"

"But you are the only student in the class who carries a guitar!"

My guitar? so what if I carry one?

"Since you carry it... you know how to play it right? We thought that you could be the musician in the party..."

"I don't play the guitar"

"Then why do you always carry it with you?"

"I don't think that's what you should concern yourself with."

I did not want to talk to him any longer. I turned around and left the school- Forever.

As I walked my way home, I did not turn around, not even once. Even when I entered through the main door of my home, I went straight to my room. I heard various noises from my mother's room. But I did not bother to look into it. I immediately jumped on my bed after tossing away my school bag and guitar. My bed is the only place on the Earth where I can finally relax. No one to disturb me, or so i thought. My mother suddenly barged into my room and started messing up my room.

she opened up my closet and took out everything from it.

"Where is it!?"

I did not understand what she was looking for. She seemed to ask me about the location of the thing she was searching for. But I did not think that it would be right to answer her. She had an irritated look on her face. A look that scared me.

"Just where the hell is it!??"

She suddenly walked up to me and asked me with an even scarier look on her face, "You dare hide it from me!?"

Me on the other hand who did not even know what she was looking for did not understand what she meant. "What are you talking about?" I asked her in a low tone of voice.

"Don't mess with me! Just where the hell did you hide that goddamn Akihito's number!?"

Once she said that I realized why she had thought that I had hidden father's number. I gathered
up all of my strength and said," I won't give you his number just so you can burn it down"

She gave me disgusted look and shouted,"So what if I burn it!? What good will you do with the number of a dead person!"

"He is not dead!!!" I had lost my temper. I stood up tall and replied her with all my voice.

"Not dead!? A person who has been missing for 7 years!?" My mother shouted with anger.

"He is not missing! He ran away from home! Because of you!!" As i said those words my heart felt a deep agony. For as long as I can remember.... I have never seen them in a healthy relationship. They would fight everyday. As a child I never knew who was right. My elder brother never seemed to care much about them. But I knew one thing... I hated them both, and I still do. They never cared about me or Haruto.

All they ever did was quarrel with each other until father finally gave up on living together with mother. One day he suddenly came into my room, seven years ago. He woke me up and told me that he would be leaving our house forever. What he told me that day is something that I clearly remember although it has been 7 years.

"Daiki... I am going to leave this house forever. I know that you don't feel sad about it... why should you? I don't remember embracing you in my arms even once...Nor do I with Haruto... Weird isn't it? I have never fulfilled my duties as your father. Now that I am finally leaving... I thought that this is the least i can do for you. Here, keep this envelop with you. It has my number in it. Of course... You don't have to call me. I don't deserve that from you. But hear me out... When one day you finally feel like you have achieved your dream...your freedom... true love... Do call me and tell me all about it. I haven't been able to give you any of those things... but I am sure that you will find it somewhere...someday. Call me and tell me that you were able to get everything you desire although I could not do anything for you. I will wait for your call... No matter how long it takes"

Those were his last words before he left. Come to think of it, that was the first time he had properly conversed with me. His words did not make me love him though. However, the envelop which he left with me, I somehow did not want to loose it.

When my mother said that he was dead, it made me loose my temper. Although I don't love him, I did not want him dead. My mother eventually went out of my room after glaring at me for a while.

CHAPTER TWO

Ashahi Minamoto

After my mother left the room, I continued to give my brain some time off. Knowing how hard it was going to be for the rest of my life made me want to go into a deep slumber. If I were to ever give myself a party it would be the day I hear that the world is about to end. However, I don't see that day anywhere near.

As time went by, I decided to join "Enis Public College". A part of my reason was that I did not score good enough in school to join some prestigious government college. The second being, I did not want to attend a private college. I wanted to be as much independent as I possibly could. Studying in a private college would mean that I would have to rely on my mother's money. Money earned from part-time jobs would not be enough for private colleges. Which meant that "Enis Public College" was my only option. A reasonable monthly fees which I could easily pay with my own earnings from working in some cafe or at McDonald and somewhat good enough educational background. Although, the educational background did not matter to me.

Honesty, I did not want to continue with my studies any longer. On my very first day of college I managed to somehow find myself the quietest corner of the class, a corner where the only thing that I could hear was the professor's lecture. Not that I actually paid any attention to it.

Right after the class was over, I rushed over to the nearby cafe and pleaded for employment. Just as I had expected, I was rejected. I again rushed over to my next class. As soon as I entered the class, I once again secured the corner to myself before anyone else could. Just like that my first day of college was over. Nothing much happened. Just another insignificant day. On my way back home, I felt glad about not attending the farewell party.

However, the very next day was different than the usual insignificant days. A part of the reason was that I had managed to get myself a part-time job at the nearby McDonald's for a reasonable payment. Nevertheless, the second reason was unpleasing.

The boy who had followed me all the way back in the last day of my school just to make use of me as a free of cost musician happened to go the same college as me. I was immensely displeased when he approached me with a smile on his face.

"Hey Daiki! It's been a while! You attending Enis College too ? Guess we're both broke here~hehehe"

His carefree words annoyed me, although his words were not a complete lie. I did not reply him back. I carefully avoided his eyes and walked past him without bothering him. But peace was never an option. He blocked my way and insisted for my reply. Not that he directly told me to reply to him; his eyes begged for my attention.

"What do you want from me?", I said in a soulless tone.

"Wow... the way you say it makes me feel like I am violating you or something. Guess you haven't changed much since high school"

"If you are done then excuse me"

"Wait. Let me tell you my name first... You don't know it, right?

His words were true. Back in school and even now in college, I don't talk with anyone. My hatred for this world and its people keep me to myself. So I did not know anyone's name back in school. Nor do i know anyone's in college.

"I am Ashahi Minamoto", he said with a smile,"Lets get along together"

"Daiki Nakamura... have no intentions of getting along with anyone", I walked past him with a heartless expression.

However, despite my heartless remarks, he continued to walk up to me at the end of every class and each time asked me some kind of silly question.

"This class was so hard right!?"

"This teacher was weird~"

"English classes are the worst right!?"

"Maybe we should have given up on studies?"

" Wanna go to the cafeteria?"

To sum it up,

His presence annoyed me.

By the end of the 3rd class, I had lost my temper as I shouted right on his face, "Stop with your nonsense already! Can't you see that you are bothering me!? If you've got time to irritate me then go and utilize that time to do something else!" I expected him to be sad. But I was taken aback by the expression on his face. His eyes looked at me with a coldness as he replied ," Don't you think that you are being immature?"

His words made no sense to me but I could not conclude it as a joke either. He came closer to me, grabbed my hand

and dragged me with him to the cafeteria where it was only us.

"Daiki... you can't stay the way you are right now! Can't you see that you are wasting your life!?"

His words sounded desperate. The look of worry in his eyes and the painful strain in his voice were all too sudden for me as I wondered to myself if he really was the cheerful boy who had been gleefully talking just a while ago. He seemed like a different person, one that I was unfamiliar with. But despite everything, I did not understand what he meant when he said that I was wasting my life. Now that I think about it, maybe I did know what he meant... But my heart could not accept it

"Daiki... listen to me... You need to start living properly. The way you are right now is not alright at all!"

"You are wrong", I replied," I think that your way of living is much worse than mine."

"Daiki... You need to stop being like that"

"You are speaking nonsense..."

"You need to start truly living"

"Shut Up!"

He stopped speaking. I did not want to stay near him any longer. As i turned around he said with a painful tone, "You are lonely aren't you...?"

I don't know when or how... but as I heard him speak, I could not move.

" I don't know the truth of your life... I don't know what you've been through... I don't know what it is that you desire either... But its painful... To see you the way you are right now is painful. It has always been painful, ever since I first saw you in the darkest corner of the classroom with your head held down in thoughts unknown to me... I don't think that I can take that loneliness away from you... If I could then I would have done that way earlier... even sincc I saw you in that corner, all alone, by yourself. I realized that I am not brave enough to do that all by myself. I am weak... scared...fragile... not someone who can heal others. I hope that you meet someone who can heal you in my place."

I was completely frozen as I heard his voice brush across the deepest corners of my heart.

CHAPTER THREE

The smile unknown

Ever since that day, Ashahi and I never talked with each other. We would avoid eye contact. In the rare occasion that our eyes did meet, we would both look away immediately.

To be honest, I was relieved.

After college I would go to my part-time job at the McDonald store. Since it was right by my college, I would go there right after getting out. It was not rare for me to skip a few classes and quietly lie down under the giant cherry tree right behind the main campus. But one day, I felt different.

Instead of heading to my regular rendezvous spot, I went to the old storeroom of the main campus. It was in the corner-most part of the cafeteria. No one ever went there, a complete soulless zone.

After the English professor had finished giving her daily lecture, I went to that storeroom with my guitar. I carried my guitar everywhere with me no matter what. I did not have any particular reason for doing that.

As I carefully opened the rusted door of the run down room a bunch of spiders escaped out with great speed. I was not afraid of them. I entered the dark room with rather reckless steps and sat at the darkest corner where no light from the only window of that room could reach me. For a while all I did was stare into the space.

Then suddenly, memories of my past flooded into my mind. They came in without any warning. It was not new to me. The memories of my past like to visit me whenever I am alone all by myself. Ever since that day when Ashahi told me those words, my mind has been a mess. I hate him for that.

The images of my gone father, the silhouette of my unbothered mother and the reflection of myself in the mirror looking at me with no emotion, everything kept on flooding into my head. And then came in my hatred, hatred for everything, hatred for everyone...

Subconsciously, I started to play my guitar. Every string I hit represented all my feelings. The melody I played was something I despised from the bottom of my heart.

Then suddenly, I was blinded by a light.

A light that came from the opened door of the storeroom. I had made sure to close the door before coming inside. I quickly stood up to discover a girl standing at the door. I could not see her face against the light.

"Why are you here?", I asked with no intention of knowing who she was. To me she was nothing more than a impediment to me spending time with myself.

"The melody you just played... I heard it"

Her voice was unusually calm, but not to me.

"So?", I said in an irritating tone.

"It was beautiful!"

Suddenly her calming voice changed into a high pitched voice. I did not know how to react to her sudden exclamation.

"I heard it from outside! You must be a really good guitarist right!?"

She started walking up to me.

"I have always liked guitars!"

She came closer-

"The melody you played was beautiful!"

She came closer-

"And I want to hear more of it!"

Until she finally reached me and said,

"But it was sad..."

Her words suddenly overwhelmed me with emotions beyond description.

"It was so sad that I could not help but come in... every string you hit was screaming... it was screaming for someone... for someone to come and comfort you"

Her words were beyond my understanding. The tune I played was calling for someone?

"You see... I thought I you were probably... you know... like... sad...like... you know right... with some tears... Like..."

I did not how to respond to her stuttering words which were irritating.

"I don't understand what you mean. If you are done then do me a favor and leave me alone already. You are annoying me", I said with coldness.

"Okay! I guess I did bother you...", She walked out from the door with swift steps. Just as she went out, she turned around with a smile on her face and said,

"I really did love your way of playing the guitar!"

This time I could finally clearly see her face... Brown hair that shined under the light and black eyes which shined brightly... She was someone who belonged to a world different from mine. I could never smile like that-

CHAPTER FOUR

To be needed

I could not remember the last time I had smiled.

Happiness is something unknown to me. It is something which I have never had ever since I can remember.

The tune which I play is never a happy one. I sing myself to sleep while desperately hitting the strings of my guitar. Maybe because my guitar is the only thing which accompanies me in those starless nights, I can't seem to leave it behind.

The melody which I hated from the core of my heart had brought a smile on that girl's face. At first I tried to not overthink it. However, as she left, her words kept on spiraling around in my head.

""But it was sad...""

How could she have known just by hearing it? The tune I play is something which I hate, but it does not necessarily sound gloomy.

Then I suddenly realized that I was being late for my part time job. I quickly went out to do my shift. I had just barely made it in time. It was compulsory for the employees in that particular shop to wear their official uniforms which was a pain to deal with. As I entered in a hurry, I quickly changed into my uniform and got to work. I had barely avoided getting scolded that day. All the other co-workers there had foul personalities. None of them were worth talking to. The owner of the shop was not particularly someone I admired either.

Just like any other day, customers started pouring into the shop. My job was to take orders. As I Continued with my work I was suddenly taken aback by that voice which said,

"1 iced coffee please"

As I looked up to glance at the face of the person to whom that voice belonged to, I realized that it was that girl...

She looked at me and recognized me immediately. With yet another smile she exclaimed,

"It's you! We met a while ago! So your work he-"

"Shh!", I said in a whispering tone,"Don't shout so loudly."

"Why though?"

"Don't ask anything for now. 1 iced Coffee. Anything else?"

"No. That's it!"

"Okay. Go sit in an empty seat. Next please!"

Surprisingly, she was quite obedient to my words. Without bothering me anymore, she went away once she was served with her order.

After working for my shift I finally took a breath of relief. I slowly got changed and headed out with my guitar, although I had no intention of returning back home where my presence was clearly not welcomed.

I went to the nearby convenience store and bought three instant ramens which would be me my dinner for that day and the breakfast for the following day.

"Anything else?", The cashier said with a smile. I was annoyed. I had already seen enough smiles for that day.

"No", I said with a soulless voice.

"Please come again"

As I headed out with my ramen, suddenly, I was stopped. Someone had held my hand. I turned around to find that girl once again. This time too, she had that smile on her face.

"We keep running into each other don't we... umm... you see...I need a little help..."

"Huh...?"

"You see... I don't have enough money with me right now and there is something I want to buy... will you lend me some money!!?"

"How much?", I said with no curiosity.

"About... 200 yen..."

I had no intention of helping her. From the very beginning of day she had been annoying me. Interrupting my time with my guitar, reminding me of memories I want to erase and now asking me for money, I had already had enough of her.

"Thank you!!!"

A wind blew past me as I stood right in front of her, outside the store.

"I will be sure to repay you tomorrow"

I looked at her hands holding a small bag full of groceries, and then at her smile which peeked at me with a blinding brightness.

"See you tomorrow!!!"

She waved me a goodbye and left.

I could not tell her...

I could not tell her that her presence was annoying me. Neither could I simply walk away when she asked for my help from me. At the end, I could not do what my mind kept on telling me-

As I walked back home I could feel my heart racing a bit faster than usual. I had never felt that way before.

Then I suddenly realized, I felt a feeling which I had always been longing for. The feeling of satisfaction... the feeling of being needed-

CHAPTER FIVE

Lies

As I went back home, I once again went straight up to my room without bothering about all the noises that kept on coming from my mother's room. To me, it was nothing new.

As soon as I entered my room I heard a very familiar voice.

"Instant ramen... not a very healthy dinner you know"

As I looked up I saw him with an unusually laid back countenance.

It was Haruto. He was sitting on my bed with the usual unbothered look in his eyes.

Haruto is my older brother. He is seven years older than me. Just like me, he is an overlooked child. We were both never loved by anyone. We both shared the same fate... However, he is different from me. Although we shared the same pain, we never actually shared it.

We never talk with each other, not even on rare occasions.

Ten years ago-

Back then... I was someone who cried over every little things. As my parents would start to raise their voices against each other, I would creep in a corner of my room. In those days, Haruto never came to me. Whenever I would peek into his room, he would be casually sitting in his bed with his ears covered with earphones. As I grew up, I started to hate the world. As he grew up, He started to feel the world. But I never actually hated him-

Around 7 years ago, a month after my father had left... that was when I started to hate him.

I had found out that he had got the exact same number from father like me that very night.

"Oh... I burned that paper", is what he said to me when I first asked him about it. I should not have cared about it if that's where he would have ended his sentence. But he continued to say,

"You should burn it too. That piece of paper is not going to get you anywhere. For us... there is nothing left to gain or loose anymore. Holding onto that paper will only result in your own misery"

Maybe his words were true. Maybe I knew it as well. And yet... I wanted to believe.

I wanted to believe in the possibility of me finding something important to me. His w
ords were like stabs of knives to my heart.

The present:

"You surprised to see me?"

Haruto looked at me with an unusual look in his eyes.

"Why are you here?", I asked.

"What a horrible thing to say to your own brother..."

"Don't beat around the bush", I said,"If you have no work here then go away already. You are being an-"

Before I could complete my sentence... I was silenced.

"You still have this paper huh?"

I looked at his hands holding a piece of paper which was none other than the paper which father had left me with.

"How did you get that!?", I shouted.

"Now now, Its not like I am about to throw this away or something"

"Where did you get it!?"

I was furious. But more than anything I was worried that he would do something to even that tiniest bit of hope that was left with me.

"Don't worry. I won't burn this or give it to mother. No wonder mother could never find this paper in your room before. Afterall, who would have thought of checking inside this old and almost rotten wooden box underneath the mattress of your bed."

"How did you know it was there?"

"Telepathy maybe. I am your brother afterall"

"Don't you dare call me your brother"

"What a harsh thing to say..."

"Give that paper to me right now and go out of my room!"

He finally stood up and got down from my bed.

"Daiki... don't you think thats its already enough"

His words made no sense but his eyes, the look in his eyes gave off a familiar feeling.

"What do you mean by its already enough?", I asked.

"You need to stop being so immature already."

"If what you're trying to tell me is to get rid of that paper then don't even bother telling that to me. I have no intention of burning it like you"

I expected him to answer me with his usual arrogant tone of voice. But what followed was silence. The look in his eyes were almost as if he was pitying me.

"Why are you staring at me with that expression!?",it was the same way in which Ashahi looked at me that day,"Why does everyone look at me like that!? Stop with those looks of pity in your eyes!"

Haruto finally spoke,
"Daiki... stop lying to yourself already"

"Me? Lying to myself?"

"Can't you see?"

"How can you possibly know what I am doing!? You never cared about me to begin with! And now you suddenly come to me and say that I am lying to myself!? Don't mess with me! Go out right now!"

This time he walked upto me and gave me my piece of paper.
"Now get out!", I shouted.

He walked up to the door and yet just stood there without leaving. He turned around once again and spoke in a low tone, "Daiki... Do you really hate everything and everyone?"

I kept silent for a while before saying,"I do. I hate everyone and everything. And that includes you. Now get out of my ro-"

"That's a lie Daiki"

Before I could finish my sentence he declared my words as a mere lie.

"Shut up! What do you know about me anyways!?"

"Daiki... you know and understand it very well. And the proof of that is the piece of paper in your hand. You need to figure out what you feel and stop being a total idiot. If you like anything, never let go of it"
He said that and left immediately.

As he left my mind became all foggy.

To be honest, I knew that his words were true. I knew that it was a lie all along. I knew that me telling myself that I hate everyone was just a way for me to escape from reality. Me crying myself to sleep at night... crying because I loved this cruel world which is full of wonders... I never hated it.

It was a lie.
A lie I made up.
A lie that I continuously told myself.
Me sitting in the darkest corner of the class... I chose it for myself.
Making myself beleive that I did not belong here... I did it to myself.

I was the reason for my sufferings all along.

That night I could not go to sleep.

CHAPTER SIX

Silhouette That Stays

When Ashahi walked up to me, why did I not realize it?

When I cried myself to sleep, why did I not realize?

When I blamed everyone, why did I not realize?

How did I not realize that It was me who was the reason for my agony?

I did not know how to feel while all these thoughts were circling through my head. It was all a mess in which no one could sort out what was me and what was my demons.

"Why are you spacing out so much today?"

"Huh?"

I looked in front of me and it was that girl. She was looking at me with her eyes sparking.

"From the morning you seem really troubled. Did something happen yesterday?"

I did not know what to say so I remained silent. My thoughts were driving me insane, That was when she held my hand and gave me something. It was 200 yen. I looked at her smiling face which was too bright for me.

"Here's your 200 yen. Thank you for helping me out yesterday! Umm... is there something on my face?..."

I realized that I had been staring at her too much. But words refused to come out of me.

"You are really quite today... If there is something in your mind you can say it to me. I will try my best to make you feel better"

"I-"

"Aisha!! Wanna come to the canteen with me!?"

Just as I was about to speak, I was interrupted.

"Canteen? Sure! Umm... Daiki, you wanna come too?"

I nodded my head to show her my wish to not go with her.

"Ok... But if something really is bothering you do speak with me, Okay?"

She left after saying those words. I stood there, all alone. Suddenly my emotions started going wild. I rushed towards the old storeroom with my guitar. I hurriedly shut myself in and immediately started playing the melody which I played everyday. It calmed me down a bit.

I saw in front of me a silhouette. It was standing and listening to the melody which I was playing. It was listening to my sadness, my pain, my agony. I hated the melody which I was playing from the bottom of my heart. But I loved the fact that the silhouette was listening to what I played. It listened to the melody which was to me the story of my life.

The story of my pathetic self lying to myself. I looked up at the shadow. It had a smile on it's face.

The image of that girl flashed right before my eyes. I tried to reach it. But it was once again... a lie. She was not really there. No matter how much I tried to reach for it, I could not. The world in which she lived in was different from mine. She was a normal girl.

One day she will fall in love with someone. Then they will have a happy marriage and she will soon become a loving mother. Me on the other hand; I will forever remain here in this darkness. There is no way that leads to hope. Everyone will eventually walk away from me.

You can't really blame anyone for leaving if you didn't do anything to make them stay.

But broken things like me and better off alone.

I wonder how I am going to live.

Regretting?

Questioning?

Apologizing?

Hating myself?

If someone asked me to name the things i love,

How long will it take me to say myself? Will I ever say it?

I wonder how my life will sound when it is told to someone? Will they take it as an example and avoid living like me? Of course they will.

I am not strong just because I know my weakness. It just makes me weaker.

I am not fearless because I am yet to learn to recognize illusion from reality.

I am not a lover just because I have felt the hate.

I am too afraid to laugh because I have known my sadness for too long.

And I am afraid that If I abandon my agony, nothing will be left of me. I will be just a walking corpse with no soul.

And yet, I wish this sadness could leave me... just like my father did.

All this while, the silhouette was still there right in front of me. It listened to every thought of mine.

"You can leave... You don't have to listen to these words circling through my head."

The silhouette did not leave.

"I told you to go away! Why are you still here!? "

The smile on the shadow's face disappeared. It turned away from me and started walking away.

That's right. That's what I deserve.

"Daiki... stop lying to yourself already"

I turned around and saw Haruto.

"Daiki... Do you really hate everything and everyone?"

"I do"

-I don't...

"Do you really want the shadow to leave?"

"I do"

-I don't...

"Are you really okay with lying to yourself?"

"I am"

-I am not...

"Are you really fine with staying trapped here in this darkness forever?"

"I am"

-I am not...

"The more you lie, the more it will hurt"

"Why do you care? You don't love me"

"No... It's you who does not love yourself"

I stopped playing the guitar. Everything was gone. The silhouette, Haruto, everything...

I looked around. There was no one. All I could hear was my own heart beat.

"If you like anything, never let go of it"

Haruto's words were ringing in my head. No matter what I did, it would not stop ringing.

"If I like anything..."

That was when I saw it, that girl with a smile on her face.

"If I like anything... I should never let go of it..."

But do I deserve that happiness? Do I deserve to live in the world which I had convinced myself to hate? Do I

deserve to live?
Do I deserve to smile as well...?

CHAPTER SEVEN

To be free

I stayed in the storeroom for a long time. The entire time i kept on questioning myself; Questions with no answers.

As I walked out of the storeroom I saw the sky in an orange shade looking down on me. I had lost track of time. It was too late to go to McDonald's and I knew that going there would only tire me out more. Not going would mean a cut in my salary which was already too little to pass a month with.

But I did not care.

I went to get my bag from the room. But as I went inside I saw her sitting right by my seat.

"So you are here! I was so worried about you!"

She hurried up to me with a look of worry in her eyes. No one had ever looked at me that way... No... That's a lie.

It was me who had failed to realize their concern for me.

"I am glad that you are alright. When I came in I saw your bag here but I could not find you anywhere. The storeroom was locked from inside... were you in there?"

I nodded.

"I see... " She looked at me with a smile.

I wanted to ask her why she was still there? Why was she waiting for me? Why did she worry about me?

"How can you smile so easily?"

"Huh?"

That was not what I wanted to ask her. But my lips moved on their own.

"I wonder what it feels like to smile like that..."

That was the first time I had felt her quietness.

"That's a difficult question that you've asked me."

I looked at her, her eyes were looking down at the ground.

"Do you see me like that? I guess so. You are not wrong. I do smile very often. It's not like I have a reason to not cry. But I choose not to... You see... everyone has a part of themselves they don't show others. You have one too right?"

"I... I do"

"Do you want to see that side of me?"

This time, She was looking directly into my eyes. The more She looked at me, the more I refused to take my eyes off her. I wanted to see how she saw me... I wanted to see the world from her eyes...

"I want to know everything about you"

I subconsciously said those words. What followed was silence. I looked at the tinge of red that spread over her cheeks. I wonder how my face looked back then. Was it the same as her? The silence was too strong for me to bear.

"Will you tell me everything about you?", I asked her. She looked up at me with tears in her eyes.

"Why... why are you crying?"

"I know right... Don't I look pathetic right now? After all, this is the first time anyone has ever said that to me. Want to know everything about me? Jeez... Do you read a lot of romance manga or something?"

"Huh? Did it sound weird!? I guess so... to suddenly hear someone say that might have been creepy... umm... I should have framed my sentence in a better way ... Or maybe-"

She busted into laughter.

"Why... why are you laughing suddenly?"

"Why? Well... I haven't seen you this flustered ever! You look so funny!"

"Huh!? I do?"

"YA... And you are all red"

"So are you"

Once again, silence took over. However, this time we did not dare look at each other.

"A...am i ...?"

"y..yes..."

"I .. I see... Umm... It's almost evening... I think I should leave now", she hurriedly took her bag and ran away.

I stood there.

"What... what was that?... Why... why am I shaking so much?"

That was the first time I had ever acted like that in front of anyone. As she left, I realized something very important...

"If you like anything, never let go of it"

I ran after picking up my bag. I ran with all that I had. I ran towards the direction my heart felt like. And then... I found her. I found her at the bridge looking down at the water beneath it. The red on her cheeks was not gone yet. I had ran a lot and yet, I was not tired at all. I walked up to her. Once she noticed me walking towards her, she did not move. Her eyes were unsteady as she looked at the water.

"I... I was serious when I said that I wanted to know all about you!"

She did not reply.

"I realized... I realized that you are important to me! And so, I can't let you go! If I do... I am going to be stuck in there... In that darkness... I don't want to feel that way anymore. I am tired... Tired of lying to myself. There's no way that I can turn back time now... all these regrets piled up in my heart make me feel sick. Anymore and I will be as good as dead. So, I don't want to regret letting you go!"

I looked at her. She looked at me and said,

"f you want... I will... I will tell you all about me... But!... Tell me all about yourself too..."

"I will! I will tell you all about me!"

We looked at each other.

And that was when,

I felt free.

Free from all the lingering thoughts that had piled up inside of me. Free from all the lies which I had made myself believe. Free from the sadness which had taken over my sanity. That was when I decided to let go of my grief. It did not make me a living corpse as now, I was more than just a soul waiting for its death. She was the reason for my happiness. Haruto was the reason that I managed to grasp that happiness. Ashahi was the reason that I first started questioning my lies.

I am grateful to all of them.

I don't hate the world after all!

I realized, someone like me can be happy as well.

Someone like me can now finally be grateful to others.

Someone like me can now finally love myself.

CHAPTER EIGHT

The first photo

" Aisha..."

I looked at her face which was staring at me for quite a while now. Her eyes were as bring as ever. She smiled at me and asked,"Why do you have that camera with you today?"

I was carrying a camera with me. I looked at my hands holding it pointing at her. It was something I did subconsciously.

"I bought this camera yesterday... I bought it with my savings. I... I wanted to click your picture with this", I said.

Her smile grew brighter as she said, "Want me to pose for you then!?"

"Yes...", I said, with a smile. That's right. I now knew how to smile because I was not alone anymore. Whenever I would open my eyes, I would see her with her usual bright smile. It had become something I loved seeing more than my guitar. I used to hate my music. But at some point, I saw that same tune bring a smile on her face. So I continued to play it.

She was looking at the water under the bridge. Her eyes were shining and her hair was curled up so beautifully... And her smile... I clicked it.

"Huh? Did you just click my photo?"

"I did"

"But I did not pose, did I ? Did it turn out good?"

"Who knows"

"Huh! Show it to me!"

"Don't wanna"

Conversations like those... I never thought I could experience something like that. Every moment that I spent with her, I wanted it to last forever.

"Daiki... it's been two months since we started dating..."

"It has been two months. Why?"

"No... I just... I just thought that this was kinda unexpected"

"What do you mean?"

"I mean... who would have thought that you would confess to me? You looked so distant from everyone... and then again... who would have thought that I would have fallen this deeply in love with you..."

"Your cheeks are red"

"Are they!?"

"No"

"Jeez... don't tease me!"

I held her hand.

"Wh...What are you doing!?"

"See. Now you are really red"

"Huhhuhh!!!!"

I wanted to never let go of her hand.

"Will you stay with me like this... forever?", I looked at her as she said those words to me.

"I will"

She looked up at me.

"I will stay with you forever! Even after we graduate! Even after we become office workers! Even after we grow old!", I said with all my heart.

"Jeez... you really do read a lot of romance novels don't you."

Her smile was precious to me.

"Aisha... after we graduate... will you marry me?". I don't know what I asked that so suddenly.

I had already told her everything about me. The fact that I had an elder brother, the fact that my relationship with my mother was not good and the fact that my father had left us all behind. She had accepted all of it. She accepted all of my past and loved my present. So I wanted to devote all of my future to her. I looked at her. She was looking at me with warmth.

"Marry you? Obviously I will!"

I felt happy. I never thought that such happiness would be a part of me.

Just like that, we reached the second year of our college. I had saved up as much money as much I could. With that money, I had bought a ring. I wanted to give it to her on our 1 year proposal anniversary. And with that, I wanted to call him. The number which my father had left behind with me... I wanted to call him and tell him that I had found the greatest happiness ever. I wanted to tell him that I was now satisfied with the way my life was. I wanted to tell him that I still hate him but am grateful to him. If it weren't for the envelop that he had left with me, I wouldn't have tried to reach my happiness. That envelop was my hope. Hope that I would someday be so happy that I would be able to call him.

As me and Aisha walked out of a store, I held her hand.

"Did something happen?", she asked me.

"Nothing"

"Really...?"

I stopped walking and pulled the ring out of my pocket. She looked at it with amazement.

I pulled her closer and put the ring in her ring finger.

"Today is our 1 year proposal anniversary... I wanted to give this ring to you today"

I looked at her. She had tears in her eyes but a smile on her face. But she said nothing. She came closer and kissed me on my cheek. That was not the first time she had done that but it took me by surprise.My heart started beating faster than ever.

"You are all red", she said in a whispering tone in my ears.

I was truly flustered. But for some reason I busted into laughter.

"Did I say something funny?", she asked me as I was almost tearing up with laughter.

"No... it's just that... Your whispers are creepy"

"Huh!? What is that supposed to mean!"

"Why should I say?"

I walked forward before her and turned around to continue laughing. At that point my stomach was almost starting to heart. But when I looked at Aisha, she was looking at me as if something wrong was about to happen. She started running at me.

"Daiki! Look Out!!"

"Look out?"

The very next moment... I was suddenly feeling really warm. I felt my self lying down in a warn pool... It was hurting for some reason... I could barely see Aisha who was crying and shouting for help. She was calling someone in a hurry... and... that's all I saw. After that I could not see anything. It was dark all around me. The warm pool around me slowly grew colder and colder.

And that was the very last thing that I remembered before losing all my senses.

CHAPTER NINE

Paralyzed

"He was hurt pretty badly by the truck. It has damaged his knee joints and fractured his legs. Luckily he will not remain paralyzed forever. However, right now he in in coma. He won't be able to move or talk. "

Huh?... I am... paralyzed?

"When will he wake up doctor!?"

Is that Haruto's voice... he sounds... so worried...

"I am afraid I can not tell that. There's no way for me to know. there have been cases where people haven't been able to wake up at all"

"No! That can't be!"

Huh?... this is Aisha's voice... she sounds so sad...

"I am not saying this to worry you all. As a doctor it is my responsibility to take care of my patient. However, I must prepare you for the worst case scenario as well. We doctors can never give false hope to our patient's family members."

I hear a crying voice... is this Aisha's?... why... why is she crying?

"Doctor... please look after my brother..."

Haruto...

"I will work my hardest."

I can hear someone walking out of the room...

"Aisha..."

"I will stay here with him a little longer"

"I see... please go home before it gets too dark"

Did Haruto left? He did... I can't hear him anymore... I don't hear that doctor either... all that I can hear is Aisha's crying voice. I ever wanted to make her cry like this.

"Daiki... please... stay with me"

I can't move at all!... dammit!... Aisha! I am right here! Please stop crying!... This... this is all my fault...

"I will come to see you everyday... until you wake up..."

I don't remember anything after that. I lost track of time long ago. All that I know is that I am paralyzed and currently in a coma. But for some reason, I can hear everything around me. I heard the door of my room opening. Just by the footsteps I knew, it was Aisha.

"Daiki... I am here again today"

It is all my fault...

"You see... I will never stop coming until you wake up... so wake up as fast as you can"

If only I hadn't met you... If only I hadn't been careless... If only I never existed... You wouldn't have had to go through this pain.

"There are so many things that I want to tell you..."

It is all my fault...

"I hope that you don't blame yourself for everything."

It's all my fault...

"I will always love with everything that I have... so... please don't blame yourself after waking up."

If only I hadn't met her...

"I will come again tomorrow..."

She never came again. I was relieved. I never wanted her to see me again. It was all my fault. It was my fault for beveling that I could escape this darkness. By believing in what was not possible, I ended up dragging Aisha into all of this. It's better this way. It's better if she eventually forgets me. It's better if she removes me from her heart. In that way, she won't feel sad anymore. I don't want her to feel that sadness because of me...

After a few days, I could finally open my eyes. This time I knew it for sure. Aisha was no longer visiting me. I was relieved. It's better that way. Eventually I started my rehabilitation once I fully gained my consciousness. That's when I found out that I had been in coma for two months.

I did not care. I had once again fallen into the same hole from which I had escaped. My nightmares once again started to haunt me. But that day... what I saw that day made me realize something horrible...

I was walking through the hospital. Because of my rehabilitation I had been able to walk pretty well. That was when I came across a dustbin. It seemed untouched for quite a while and in it was a newspaper. I took it out because something intrigued me. I opened it and saw it.... The most horrible and terrifying murder case in the past 7 decades of Japan's history... The murder case of 19 years old Aisha Shiratorizawa, a student of 'Enis Public College'. The murderer was a japanese mafia gang member who ruthlessly forced the young girl into the darkness of a deserted lane... harassed her and in the end... decapitated her body into countless peices with a chainsaw... The girl was supposedly returning home from the City general hospital... All the pieces of her body couldn't be found even after hours of searching...

"huh... HA...HAHAHAHAHA! So that's what happened... huh... uhhuh... AHHHH!...H...Of Course that's what happened!... She was sucked into the darknes... Anyone who comes in contact with my darkness will have the same outcome! HUH....she...she died...I see... I get it... I get that I have no right to be happy! I get it very well that..."

"I hate everything"

Printed by Libri Plureos GmbH in Hamburg,
Germany